A Needle for a Needle
A Mother's Covid Revenge

A Novella by
Vernon Coleman

Books by Vernon Coleman include:

Medical
The Medicine Men
Paper Doctors
Everything You Want To Know About Ageing
The Home Pharmacy
Aspirin or Ambulance
Face Values
Stress and Your Stomach
A Guide to Child Health
Guilt
The Good Medicine Guide
An A to Z of Women's Problems
Bodypower
Bodysense
Taking Care of Your Skin
Life without Tranquillisers
High Blood Pressure
Diabetes
Arthritis
Eczema and Dermatitis
The Story of Medicine
Natural Pain Control
Mindpower
Addicts and Addictions
Dr Vernon Coleman's Guide to Alternative Medicine
Stress Management Techniques
Overcoming Stress
The Health Scandal
The 20 Minute Health Check
Sex for Everyone
Mind over Body
Eat Green Lose Weight
Why Doctors Do More Harm Than Good
The Drugs Myth

Complete Guide to Sex
How to Conquer Backache
How to Conquer Pain
Betrayal of Trust
Know Your Drugs
Food for Thought
The Traditional Home Doctor
Relief from IBS
The Parent's Handbook
Men in Bras, Panties and Dresses
Power over Cancer
How to Conquer Arthritis
How to Stop Your Doctor Killing You
Superbody
Stomach Problems – Relief at Last
How to Overcome Guilt
How to Live Longer
Coleman's Laws
Millions of Alzheimer Patients Have Been Misdiagnosed
Climbing Trees at 112
Is Your Health Written in the Stars?
The Kick-Ass A–Z for over 60s
Briefs Encounter
The Benzos Story
Dementia Myth
Waiting

Psychology/Sociology
Stress Control
How to Overcome Toxic Stress
Know Yourself (1988)
Stress and Relaxation
People Watching
Spiritpower
Toxic Stress
I Hope Your Penis Shrivels Up
Oral Sex: Bad Taste and Hard To Swallow
Other People's Problems

The 100 Sexiest, Craziest, Most Outrageous Agony Column
Questions (and Answers) Of All Time
How to Relax and Overcome Stress
Too Sexy To Print
Psychiatry
Are You Living With a Psychopath?

Politics and General
England Our England
Rogue Nation
Confronting the Global Bully
Saving England
Why Everything Is Going To Get Worse Before It Gets Better
The Truth They Won't Tell You...About The EU
Living In a Fascist Country
How to Protect & Preserve Your Freedom, Identity & Privacy
Oil Apocalypse
Gordon is a Moron
The OFPIS File
What Happens Next?
Bloodless Revolution
2020
Stuffed
The Shocking History of the EU
Coming Apocalypse
Covid-19: The Greatest Hoax in History
Old Man in a Chair
Endgame
Proof that Masks do more harm than Good
Covid-19: The Fraud Continues
Covid-19: Exposing the Lies
Social Credit: Nightmare on Your Street
NHS: What's wrong and how to put it right
They want your money and your life.
Their Terrifying Plan

Diaries and Autobiographies
Diary of a Disgruntled Man

Just another Bloody Year
Bugger off and Leave Me Alone
Return of the Disgruntled Man
Life on the Edge
The Game's Afoot
Tickety Tonk
Memories 1
Memories 2
Memories 3
My Favourite Books

Animals
Why Animal Experiments Must Stop
Fighting For Animals
Alice and Other Friends
Animal Rights – Human Wrongs
Animal Experiments – Simple Truths

General Non Fiction
How to Publish Your Own Book
How to Make Money While Watching TV
Strange but True
Daily Inspirations
Why Is Public Hair Curly
People Push Bottles Up Peaceniks
Secrets of Paris
Moneypower
101 Things I Have Learned
100 Greatest Englishmen and Englishwomen
Cheese Rolling, Shin Kicking and Ugly Tattoos
One Thing after Another

Novels (General)
Mrs Caldicot's Cabbage War
Mrs Caldicot's Knickerbocker Glory
Mrs Caldicot's Oyster Parade
Mrs Caldicot's Turkish Delight
Deadline

Second Chance
Tunnel
Mr Henry Mulligan
The Truth Kills
Revolt
My Secret Years with Elvis
Balancing the Books
Doctor in Paris
Stories with a Twist in the Tale (short stories)
Dr Bullock's Annals
The Awakening of Dr Amelia Leighton
A Needle for a Needle

The Young Country Doctor Series
Bilbury Chronicles
Bilbury Grange
Bilbury Revels
Bilbury Country
Bilbury Village
Bilbury Pie (short stories)
Bilbury Pudding (short stories)
Bilbury Tonic
Bilbury Relish
Bilbury Mixture
Bilbury Delights
Bilbury Joys
Bilbury Tales
Bilbury Days
Bilbury Memories

Novels (Sport)
Thomas Winsden's Cricketing Almanack
Diary of a Cricket Lover
The Village Cricket Tour
The Man Who Inherited a Golf Course
Around the Wicket
Too Many Clubs and Not Enough Balls

Cat books
Alice's Diary
Alice's Adventures
We Love Cats
Cats Own Annual
The Secret Lives of Cats
Cat Basket
The Cataholics' Handbook
Cat Fables
Cat Tales
Catoons from Catland

As Edward Vernon
Practice Makes Perfect
Practise What You Preach
Getting Into Practice
Aphrodisiacs – An Owner's Manual
The Complete Guide to Life

Written with Donna Antoinette Coleman
How to Conquer Health Problems between Ages 50 & 120
Health Secrets Doctors Share With Their Families
Animal Miscellany
England's Glory
Wisdom of Animals

Dedication
To Antoinette, my true and eternal love, who is my everyone and always will be.

Overnight, Mrs Mallory had been transported from one world to another.

In her old world she'd had a son; a young man whom she loved very much, in that unique way that a mother loves a child, and of whom she was inestimably proud. Leigh, the son in question, had been a young, healthy man with hopes, ambitions and a future.

Now, in the new world into which she had been forced, she no longer had a son.

And Leigh, once so alive and full of hope, no longer had any sort of future. He had only a past.

Through some strange trick of her memory, Mrs Mallory remembered him not as the well-built young man he had become, an athlete who played football and cricket for their local town teams, and whose picture had appeared in the paper several times in the last year (the cuttings from *The Bugle and Advertiser*, neatly clipped and smartly framed stood on the mantelpiece in the living room, one either side of her proudest material possession, the carriage clock which she'd inherited from her grandfather) but as a small boy with curly blond hair and an ever present, captivating smile. He'd lost a front milk tooth when he'd crashed on his tricycle and in the photo he had an engagingly cheeky appearance. He'd been brave after the accident, his mother remembered, and she and his Dad had replaced the tooth with not one but two fifty pence coins because of the way in which it had been lost and the quiet courage he'd shown afterwards. He'd cried, of course, but not overmuch, and an hour after the crash it had been he, with a sticking plaster on one elbow and another on a cheek, who had insisted that he get back onto his tricycle (when the front wheel had been straightened out) and resume his ride.

It has been five weeks since Leigh had died, and Mrs Mallory felt increasingly dissatisfied with the explanations she had received, both from her son's GP and from the hospital doctor who had been in charge when he had died.

She was increasingly convinced that her son had not died of 'natural causes', as the doctors both insisted, in a glib, offhand, disinterested and patronising sort of way, but had died as a result of the covid vaccination he had been given.

In her darkest moments (moments which had now begun to dominate her thinking and could, in truth, no longer be dismissed as 'moments') she was convinced that he had been murdered. She felt embarrassed by this suspicion and didn't mention it to anyone – not even to her husband.

The covid pandemic had started just over a year earlier and the Government, the medical profession, the media and the BBC had all promoted the vaccine as the solution to the threat of an infection which mathematicians said would kill untold millions and threaten the future of mankind.

Mrs Mallory had refused the covid vaccine. Saying 'No' had not been an easy decision to make since she had been working as an assistant in a care home when the vaccine had been offered. Because the vaccination had been compulsory, this had led to her losing her job. There'd been quite a lot of fuss and bother when she refused the manager's order that all the staff be jabbed.

'This isn't an invitation!' shouted the manager, an unpleasant, aggressive woman of 20 stone or more who ran the care home with an iron fist in a rubber glove and did so, it was generally admitted, with slightly less compassion and interest in her charges than someone who ran a kennels for dogs or a cattery for cats might have been reasonably expected to exhibit.

'Roll up your sleeve and be jabbed like the rest of us!' she snarled.

The manager always wore two thick cotton face masks and had to shout so that people could hear her. Unfortunately, she never spoke distinctly even when her mouth wasn't covered and the masks made it difficult to make out what she'd said.

'Well, I'm off then,' said Mrs Mallory, with quiet determination. 'I've read all about this vaccine and I don't believe it does what they say it does and I certainly don't believe it's as safe as they say it is. They've only been testing it for five minutes and I'm not having that stuff pushed into my body! Heaven only knows what it'll do to the people who have it.'

'I suppose you know better than the experts,' snapped the manager, furious because Mrs Mallory was a hard worker who not only did the work of three but was also much liked by all the residents. The manager much preferred to spend her days sitting in her office eating the steady supply of chocolates and biscuits which had been donated to the staff by relatives; a supply which was itself regularly augmented by the goodies left behind in the bedrooms of deceased patients.

'I've been doing a little research,' replied Mrs Mallory. 'I've watched videos made by a doctor who is known as the 'Old Man in a Chair' and read some articles online. It seems that it normally takes years and years to make a vaccine, and to test it thoroughly, but this one hasn't gone through all those tests. It's still just an experiment.'

'Well the Government says it's safe, the drug company says it's safe and that nice Dr Gates says it's safe – you can tell he's trustworthy because he wears pink jumpers.'

'Why does wearing a pink jumper make him trustworthy?' asked Mrs Mallory, genuinely puzzled, as she often was when the manager spoke.

'My first husband always wore a blue jumper and you couldn't trust him an inch,' said the manager firmly. 'He bought it at the Army and Navy stores and said it had been made for officers. But my second has a pink jumper from Marks and Spencer and he's utterly reliable. Even before the lockdowns started he didn't even go to the pub. He's happy to sit in front of the telly with a crate of beer beside his chair. You couldn't find a more reliable husband however hard you looked. I think you can always trust a man in a pink jumper.'

Mrs Mallory didn't say anything.

'And that lady from the drug company says it's safe!' said the care home manager, who was on something of a roll. 'I saw her being interviewed on the news. She invented the vaccine in a laboratory. She's a world-wide hero. I heard that every time she goes into a restaurant people stand up and bang their cutlery on the table. Are you saying all those people in posh restaurants don't know what they're doing? They said on the news that she went to the theatre in London and the entire cast and audience stood and cheered her to the rafters after the final curtain. And my newspaper says that the Queen is going to make her a lady. I'm not surprised. She's been on the television, talking about her new vaccine, more times than that Matt Hancock.'

'But you can't take any notice of what she says!' protested Mrs Mallory. 'She's going to make a fortune out of flogging the stuff she's invented! And that Bill Gates isn't a doctor.'

'I'm sure he could be a doctor if he wanted to be one,' said the care home manager indignantly. 'He looks like a doctor and he's really nice. The BBC thinks a lot of him.' She paused, as though this were all that needed to be said.

'He seems a bit smarmy to me,' said Mrs Mallory.

'And then there's that nice Dr Mike Rainbaugh, the doctor off the telly,' continued the manager. 'He's always on the telly. He says the new vaccine is perfectly safe and will kill the bug dead in its tracks – just like putting bleach down the loo. He says he's going to inject his wife live on television to prove how safe it is. And as soon as it's been cleared for kiddies he's going to inject them live on television too.'

'Oh, I don't trust him,' said Mrs Mallory with a shudder. 'He's very smarmy too. He uses far too much hair oil and looks too much like the salesman who sold us our last motor car. My George and I both thought he seemed really nice and he gave me a bunch of tulips when we'd paid over the money but the car's gear box went a week after we got it home and it cost us nearly £2,000 for a new one.'

'Dr Rainbaugh sold you a car?'

'No, the salesman who looked like Dr Rainbaugh.'

'Oh.'

'Besides,' continued Mrs Mallory, 'that Dr Rainbaugh does all those television adverts for crisps, draught excluders and walking sticks. How can you trust a doctor who advertises crisps, draught excluders and walking sticks? It's not right. I didn't think doctors were allowed to do things like that.'

True to her word, and firm in her view, Mrs Mallory refused to be vaccinated and left her job at the care home. The residents and other members of staff were so sad that they clubbed together and bought her a leaving card and a large bar of Toblerone chocolate. The card had a picture of a disco on the front and when you opened it a cheery voice sang Happy Birthday in three languages, one after the other. Mrs Mallory recognised the English version and thought the other two were French and German but she wasn't entirely sure, and her friend Edith said she thought one of them could have been Spanish. Mrs Mallory's best friend, who was in tears, apologised for the card and said that Mrs Jenkins, who also worked in the home but who was generally thought to be pottier than any of the patients, had purchased the card and the chocolate because she had mistakenly thought they were celebrating Mrs Mallory's birthday. Mrs Mallory, a kind woman who hated to see people get upset, said it didn't matter at all and that since she was leaving and starting a new time in her life, it was a sort of rebirth and so a birthday card was in some ways quite appropriate.

Mrs Mallory had tried, but to her great regret failed, to persuade her husband and son not to be vaccinated. She was the only member of her immediately family to refuse the vaccine.

George, Mrs Mallory's husband, had at first decided not to be vaccinated. He always liked to please his wife, whom he loved very much indeed, and he trusted her judgement on all matters, particularly in relation to food, health and what he, in his rather old-fashioned way, referred to as 'domestic matters', but in the end he had found it impossible to say 'No'.

There were two difficulties in saying 'no' to the vaccine.

First, Mr Mallory had a hip problem. Two years earlier he had developed a pain and some stiffness in his left hip. The nurse who worked with their GP had diagnosed arthritis and had prescribed some tablets. When the pills didn't do much to help him she had referred him to a consultant at the hospital. The consultant's secretary had sent Mr Mallory a note warning him that he would not be seen at the hospital unless he had a certificate showing that he'd had the covid vaccination. Meanwhile, Mr Mallory had difficulty in moving and needed a walking stick to help him get around.

Mrs Mallory had rung the hospital a couple of times but the waiting list seemed to be getting longer. When she'd telephoned the first time, the secretary had said there would be a nine month wait for an initial appointment. When she'd telephoned a second time, the secretary told her that the waiting time had gone up to fourteen months. 'How can the waiting time be getting longer?' asked Mrs Mallory, genuinely puzzled. The secretary had explained that the social distancing policies, which the hospital was following very strictly, meant that the surgeons, like many other surgeons around the country, were now only operating on one day a fortnight.

Second, Mr Mallory's employer had told him that he would be fired if he didn't produce a certificate to say that he had been vaccinated. Mr Mallory had spoken to his union representative and asked if his boss could force him to be vaccinated. The man from the union had said that it was Mr Mallory's duty to have the vaccine in order to protect his workmates, as well as himself, and that it was union policy strongly to support the management line on this issue.

'We can't afford for both of us to be out of work,' Mr Mallory said to his wife, with great sadness. 'Besides, the doctors all say it's safe and the Queen says we should all be vaccinated to protect our families and the old people.' Mr Mallory was a confirmed royalist and he believed everything the Queen said. He hated to disappoint his wife, for he felt that he was letting her down by allowing himself to be given the vaccine, but at the same time, he could not believe that the Queen would deliberately mislead him.

'And the Archbishop of Canterbury said it was our duty to have it,' he would have added, except that he and his wife didn't much talk about religion. Nor did Mr Mallory mention (because he didn't want to upset his wife) that he had heard the Archbishop say that Jesus would love people more if they were vaccinated. Mr Mallory was more of a believer than Mrs Mallory and the Archbishop's words meant a good deal to him.

And so George had trotted along to their GP's surgery where one of two nurses on duty had jabbed him with the covid-19 vaccine.

The practice was so busy giving vaccinations that there was a five week wait for proper appointments with a nurse.

(The doctors weren't available at all to see patients in the flesh. There were rumours that you could speak to a doctor on the telephone if you were insistent and lucky but Dr Burton-Summerhayes, their GP and one of the partners, had told a neighbour of Mrs Mallory's that it was important that she avoided all contact with patients so that she didn't become ill herself. The GP said that if she caught covid and became ill she wouldn't be available for her patients. Mr Mallory didn't quite understand how not seeing patients so that you would be able to see patients made sense. Nor did he understand why the doctor didn't trust the vaccine to protect her, since that was what all the doctors and all the nurses and all the politicians and all the journalists were saying. Still, there were a lot of things he didn't much understand so he didn't say anything.

Mr Mallory's wife had told him to ask which make of vaccine he was being given, and to ask for a batch number too, but when he had hesitantly asked for this information the nurse had snapped at him. She told him that they didn't have time to waste on unnecessary chit chat because they were too busy protecting people. She said it was a race against time if they were going to save the world.

The patients who had been vaccinated had to sit in the waiting room for fifteen minutes, in case they collapsed, and the man who had been behind George in the queue to be vaccinated, and who now sat next to him, said it looked as though the doctors were making quite a bundle because, although the nurses were doing the jabbing, it was the doctors who were getting the cash. He said that after counting the rate at which the jabbing was going on that he thought the doctors were making at least £1,000 an hour. 'There will be some smart new cars in the doctors' car park,' the man predicted.

Mr and Mrs Mallory's son, Leigh, had also been vaccinated.

His mother had talked to him and tried to dissuade him from being jabbed but she'd failed. And she would never forgive herself for that.

Leigh Mallory was 23-years-old and worked as a delivery driver, though he had recently found himself dreaming of going to college. He thought he would like to do something in health care, something more deeply satisfying than delivering parcels. 'Pharmacy seems a good career,' he said to his mum. 'There's no blood and you don't have to get up a night, but you're still helping people.'

'Not even doctors get up at night these days,' she reminded him, proud of his new ambition.

Leigh was an only child, and still lived at home because he couldn't afford to rent a flat of his own. The van he used for his deliveries belonged to the company he worked for but sometimes, if he worked late or had a route which ended up very close to where he lived, the boss let him drive the van home and park it in their driveway. There was just room for the van alongside his Dad's third hand Ford Mondeo.

Leigh had listened to his mum attentively when she had told him her fears about the covid-19 vaccine, but eventually he confessed (with not a little reluctance) that he was going to be jabbed because his life wasn't going to be worth living if he didn't roll up his sleeve and take the vaccine.

The local football and cricket clubs (both of which he was a keen member) had issued a notice stating that all team members would be expected to be fully vaccinated and that any member who wasn't vaccinated would not be allowed to play for any of the teams or ever attend any of the social functions. And his boss had told him that if he didn't have a certificate proving that he'd been vaccinated he wouldn't be allowed to go to work. His union representative had been rather pompous about it and had (as with his father) told him that the union fully supported the drive to get everyone vaccinated.

'Besides,' Leigh had said when the lockdowns had ended, 'a group of us are going to a Sauteed Kidneys concert in London and Rancid Reynolds, the lead singer, has announced that they'll refuse entry to anyone who hasn't got a certificate to show they've had the covid vaccination.'

Rancid Reynolds, who was one of Leigh's heroes, had also appeared in numerous print and television advertisements promoting the vaccine and had, it had been reported, been recruited as a paid Ambassador for Vaccination'.

Nevertheless, Leigh had felt bad about having the vaccine. He loved his mum very much and didn't like to disappoint her.

Leigh had been relatively fine for two days after the vaccination though he had complained of feeling very tired and having a terrible ache in his arm.

'It's nothing,' he told his parents with a shrug. 'I'm not worried. Most of the lads at work had similar symptoms. It'll wear off in a day or two.'

And then, suddenly, on the third day after the vaccination, he became seriously ill while he was at work. He'd been loading parcels into his van when he had a sudden chest pain. Leigh's heart was beating three times as fast as usual and he was very short of breath. A recorded phone message at Leigh's GP's surgery made it clear that the doctors did not deal with emergencies of any kind. A telephone call to the ambulance service didn't prove much more successful. After being told that there would be a twelve hour wait for an ambulance, Leigh's boss put his young employee into the back of one of their vans and drove him straight to the hospital.

The doctor on call at first thought that perhaps Leigh had indigestion, thought again when he'd checked his patient's pulse, and finally diagnosed a condition called myocarditis. After performing an essential PCR test (to see if Leigh had covid-19), and asking Leigh to sign a form agreeing that he did not want to be resuscitated if it looked as if he were going to die, the doctor gave him a huge injection of a benzodiazepine tranquilliser to calm him down and keep him quiet. The doctor then left Leigh on a trolley in a corridor just off the accident and emergency department and rushed off. He and all the on duty nurses all had to attend an important final rehearsal for their next Tik-Tok video (though having spent the weekend driving two hundred miles in order to hold up traffic in central London, at a protest against the use of oil) the doctor would have preferred to spend a quiet hour in the canteen with a latte, a cinnamon croissant and the nurse whom he had just persuaded to fly off with him to Bali for a long weekend as soon as their next five day strike was over. (He was privately delighted to have been able to buy the Bali tickets with the aid of the air-miles he had accumulated within the last year.)

Tragically, by the time the doctor and the nurses had finished rehearsing, and had remembered where they'd left their patient, Leigh's heart had stopped and he was dead. He had, indeed, been dead for some little while.

'We didn't need to bother with that 'Do Not Resuscitate' form,' said one of the nurses bitterly, removing the form from the clipboard attached to the rail at the side of the trolley. She stared at the form, thinking, and then said: 'If we filled in patients' names in pencil, and got them to sign in pencil, we could use the forms again if they died before we needed to use it. Over a year it would save a lot of paper.'

The doctor agreed that this was a good idea and the pair of them agreed to bring it up at the department's daily Climate and Recycling meeting later that afternoon.

Mr and Mrs Mallory had been devastated by the news of their son's untimely and unexpected death. They sat that evening in their kitchen, holding hands but saying nothing for a while. Their grief filled the room and was almost tangible.

'He was so young and so healthy,' said a puzzled Mr Mallory, eventually. He had been proud of his son's sporting achievements. 'He never had any trouble with his heart,' he added.

Mrs Mallory squeezed his hand, took another tissue from the box in front of them both and blew her nose. She took a second tissue and wiped her eyes.

'He was the fittest man in the cricket club,' said Mr Mallory. 'He could bowl unchanged for an hour.'

'I'll make us a cup of tea,' said Mrs Mallory. She had always been a believer in the medicinal and soothing properties of a nice cup of tea. And she needed to do something.

Mr Mallory nodded.

Mrs Mallory squeezed her husband's hand, disentangled her fingers and filled the kettle. 'It was that vaccine,' she said, quite suddenly, as she waited for the water to boil.

Mr Mallory looked across at her.

'That covid vaccine he had,' said Mrs Mallory. 'I saw a video with that doctor who is the Old Man in a Chair. He said that the covid vaccine was causing heart problems. Lots of fit, young adults have been dying because of it.'

'Do you really think so?' said Mr Mallory, who didn't watch internet videos, thinking that most of the stuff online was dangerous rubbish. 'There hasn't been anything about it on the news.'

'Oh, the BBC is as bent as a fish hook,' said Mrs Mallory, angrily. 'They just say what the Government tells them to say. They're all crooks. I wouldn't trust them to tell me the time.' She got two mugs out of the cupboard and put a tea bag in each, then took a container of milk out of the fridge. She turned, went back to the table, took another two tissues and blew her nose and wiped her eyes again. Then she made two mugs of tea and sat down with her husband.

'We should talk to someone about it,' said Mrs Mallory.

'Who?' asked her husband.

'Dr Burton-Summerhayes,' said Mrs Mallory. 'She was Leigh's GP.'

'OK,' said Mr Mallory. 'We'll go and see her.' Privately, he didn't think that seeing Dr Burton-Summerhayes would be very useful. It was his experience that doctors always stuck together and never took responsibility when anything went wrong. But he loved his wife very much, he had loved his son very much, and he would support his wife in anything she wanted to do.

They drank their tea and then Mrs Mallory rang the health centre where the GP worked.

'Dr Burton-Summerhayes isn't seeing patients in person,' said the receptionist. 'You can have an appointment to see the practice nurse on the 15th of next month. Or I can put you on the waiting list for a telephone appointment with Dr Burton-Summerhayes.'

'I need to see the doctor tomorrow,' said Mrs Mallory. 'It's important.'

'Oh, that wouldn't be possible at all,' said the receptionist, as though Mrs Mallory had asked for the GP to visit her at home, provide a full body massage and give her a free voucher for discounted electrical goods. 'Dr Burton-Summerhayes only comes into the health centre on Friday afternoons and then only for an hour,' explained the receptionist. 'That's when she signs her letters. She does all her work from home. It's much more time efficient and it helps ensure that the doctor doesn't catch covid by having to mix with ordinary people.'

'What time is she there on Fridays?' asked Mrs Mallory.

'Usually at a little after three,' replied the receptionist. 'She goes to a medical luncheon on Fridays.'

'A medical luncheon? What's that?'

'The drug companies take it in turns to buy the local doctors a lunch,' explained the receptionist. 'They have a lunch every weekday. On Fridays they all go to the French restaurant at the Country Club. They never finish there until just before three.'

'Thank you,' said Mrs Mallory. 'I'll see her on Friday then.'

'I'm afraid she won't see you,' said the receptionist frostily. 'Dr Burton-Summerhayes doesn't see patients in the flesh, as it were.'

'She'll see me,' said Mrs Mallory firmly, putting down the telephone and therefore missing the receptionist's protest and the automated invitation to visit the health centre's website and to leave a rating on the TruthPilot site.

'**D**r Burton-Summerhayes?'

The young woman in a light tan trouser suit, flat-heeled matching shoes and a standard health service face mask, turned and glared at Mrs Mallory who, with her husband beside her, had been sitting on a couple of uncomfortable stacking chairs in the health centre's reception area and were now both standing.

'Please speak to the receptionist,' said the woman, who had identified herself by responding when her name was called. She accompanied the instruction with an imperious wave of the hand in the direction of the space where the receptionist would have been standing if she had been there instead of in the loo replying to a text message from her sister who lived in France and was going through a particularly tedious house purchase.

'We need to speak to you, doctor,' said Mrs Mallory. 'It's very important.'

'This is a health centre, we don't deal with medical emergencies here,' said the doctor firmly. 'If you have an urgent health problem you must go to the Accident and Emergency department at the General Hospital.' She had her hair cut in the sort of short, boyish style favoured by women who swam or visited a gym on a regular basis, and who couldn't be bothered dealing with a complicated hairstyle. She wore no make-up and no jewellery and carried a black, plastic attaché case instead of a handbag. The bag looked important, as though it might contain a selection of portable medical instruments and a compendium of essential drugs. In fact the bag contained a folding umbrella and a copy of a yachting magazine. One of her partners had a small sailing boat moored in a Marina at Weymouth but Dr Burton-Summerhayes had plans to purchase something larger. She wanted something with a proper cabin, an engine and an area at the back of the boat for sunbathing. She certainly didn't want a boat with sails or ropes.

Dr Burton-Summerhayes firmly disliked being a GP, though the hours were much lighter than they had been a generation earlier, and the rewards were generous, and she had recently applied for a job as medical director of a large, well-known drug company. Her experience in general practice would, she knew, be very much in her favour. General practice didn't offer an ambitious doctor much in the way of career prospects but in the pharmaceutical industry the sky was the limit, and with bonuses and share options added onto a large salary and expense account the overall package was extraordinarily attractive. Dr Burton-Summerhayes was a very competitive woman (she had dumped her last boyfriend when she had found that her earnings exceeded his) and the drug company job should push her earnings into the stratosphere.

'It's about our son, Leigh,' said Mrs Mallory quickly. She moved to follow the doctor. 'He died earlier this week.'

'I didn't know,' said the doctor, turning slightly and automatically putting on the face that she thought made her look sympathetic, though most people who were exposed to it thought she was suffering from a bad attack of wind and merely endeavouring to prevent an embarrassing escape of flatus. 'I'm so sorry. Was he one of our patients?'

'He was. We're all your patients. Our family has been with this practice since Dr Naylor was alive.'

Dr Naylor had been an old-fashioned doctor who had smoked heavily, drunk malt whisky as though determined to single-handedly boost the profits at the distilleries on Islay, and laughingly boasted that he never ate anything that was green, except mint choc chip ice cream. He had died of a heart attack in his late fifties. The church where his funeral service was held had been overflowing with patients, relatives and others; many of them were in tears. Dr Naylor had been much mourned by patients, though not mourned or missed by his junior partners, including Dr Burton-Summerhayes, who had universally regarded him as they might have regarded a dinosaur if one had wandered into the health centre.

'Where did he die? Your son.'

'In the hospital.'

'Then I'm afraid you must collect the death certificate from them,' said Dr Burton-Summerhayes, speaking firmly and with the finality of someone equipped with the heart of a bureaucrat.

'I believe you were responsible for his death,' said Mrs Mallory loudly and equally firmly and with only the slightest hint of a tremor in her voice. 'If you don't speak to me I shall make formal complaints to the General Medical Council and the National Health Service.'

'Why do you think I might have been responsible for his death?' demanded the doctor defensively.

'You arranged for him to have the covid vaccination.'

'Oh,' said the doctor, relieved. 'You're one of those, are you? Have you been reading and listening to all the nonsense on the internet? I suppose you've been listening to the nonsense from that Old Man in a Chair!'

'Which is it to be, doctor?' asked Mrs Mallory. 'Will you give me five minutes of your time or shall I write my letters of complaint?'

The doctor sighed and tutted. 'Follow me,' she said. 'But you'll both have to put on face masks. I won't see you unless you're properly masked.' She turned and pointed once again at the reception desk. 'You'll find a box of face masks on the counter.'

A minute or two later, Mr and Mrs Mallory, properly and fully masked, sat on chairs in front of Dr Burton-Summerhayes's desk. Mr Mallory, who had difficulty in breathing at the best of times, struggled to get his breath. Dr Burton-Summerhayes sat behind the desk, leaning backwards so as to put as much distance as possible between her and the annoying couple.

'So, what nonsense have you heard?' demanded the doctor, who'd had a naturally condescending and patronising manner since she was seven-years-old.

'The doctor at the hospital told us that Leigh had a heart attack. They think he probably had myocarditis. He was a very fit young man until he had the covid vaccine.'

'I'm afraid that apparently fit young men fall down and die all the time,' said Dr Burton-Summerhayes, as though talking to a halfwit. 'There may have been an underlying abnormality that hasn't previously been identified.'

'Leigh never had any symptoms of any illness,' said Mrs Mallory. 'He had chickenpox when he was little but he never had any serious illness.'

'And why do you think that the covid vaccine might have been responsible for his death?'

'He was perfectly healthy until he had the vaccination. Then within three days he was dead.'

'Just a coincidence, I'm afraid,' said the doctor. 'If someone had a cup of coffee and was then run over by a bus would you blame the cup of coffee?'

'Of course not,' said Mrs Mallory, finding it hard not to leap across the desk and strangle the doctor. 'But there have been a lot of similar deaths,' said Mrs Mallory. 'Official statistics here and in the United States have shown a massive increase in the incidence of serious illness among healthy, young men – particularly myocarditis and heart disease.'

'You've been looking at the internet?'

'I have.'

'Do you have any medical training? Do you have a medical degree?'

'No, I've not had any formal training. No, I'm not a doctor.' Mrs Mallory didn't think it would do her cause any good to mention her experience working in a care home.

'There's a lot of nonsense on the internet,' said Dr Burton-Summerhayes. 'A very great deal of very misleading nonsense has been published and without proper training you could not be expected to understand the complexities behind the use of the covid-19 vaccine – or, indeed, any other vaccine. The authorities here, in the United States and everywhere else have all stated that the vaccine is very effective and perfectly safe. The World Health Organisation has given the covid vaccine its seal of approval. Without the vaccine there would have been many millions more deaths. I'm pleased to say that the authorities are removing from YouTube all videos which question the official, authorised point of view.'

'But it's not true that there have been a lot of covid deaths, doctor,' said Mr Mallory, pulling down his mask and speaking for the first time. Mr Mallory was a small, shy and rather gentle man. He rarely spoke up to defend himself but he would lay down his life to defend and support his wife, whom he loved very much indeed. 'I was a little sceptical, but I looked at the evidence over the last few nights,' he began, enjoying the ability to breathe without the mask. 'And I found that there is a lot of scientific evidence showing that the vaccine can cause a good many very serious illnesses.' Dr Burton-Summerhayes, who had moved her chair back as far as it would go when Mr Mallory had lowered his mask, leant back even further so that the back of her chair was touching the wall behind her.

Mr Mallory took a small notebook out of his jacket pocket and flipped over the pages. 'For one thing,' he began, 'the misuse of the PCR test has produced a massive exaggeration of the incidence of covid. Patients with cancer and heart disease have been diagnosed as covid and left untreated if they had a positive PCR test. Even people who were involved in road accidents were formally diagnosed and treated as covid patients – simply on the basis of the PCR test.'

'That's absolute nonsense,' said Dr Burton-Summerhayes, dismissively. 'I don't know where you heard that but it's nonsense. The PCR test is an approved method of diagnosing covid. But we're getting away from the point. As I understand it, you are claiming that the vaccine was responsible for your son's death. And yet there is not, and never has been, the slightest bit of evidence to sustain that argument. The covid-19 vaccine is perfectly safe and very effective.'

'But there is evidence showing that the vaccine causes serious health problems,' said Mrs Mallory. 'Even before the vaccination programmes started there was evidence that the vaccine would cause health problems,' said Mrs Mallory. 'I saw one video that was published in the autumn of 2020. 'The Old Man in a Chair' listed all the possible health problems that the vaccine could cause – and myocarditis and heart trouble were on the list.'

'Absolute poppycock! You've been listening to discredited conspiracy theorists. All Governments are advised by very experienced, well qualified medical and scientific experts who have pronounced the vaccines effective and safe.'

'In December 2020, the Old Man in a Chair read a long list of side effects published by the Food and Drug Administration in the United States of America…' began Mrs Mallory. 'And he'd been warning about the vaccine for months beforehand.'

'Oh, you haven't been listening to him, have you?' said Dr Burton-Summerhayes with an exasperated shake of her head. 'He's been shown to be a dangerous and discredited conspiracy theorist. You would be very much better off putting your trust in the experts who know about these things.'

'But most of those experts seem to have financial links with the drug companies making the vaccines,' pointed out Mrs Mallory. 'You'd hardly expect them to be critical or even independent, would you?'

'I'm not going to sit here and listen to you cast aspersions on some of the profession's most eminent people,' said Dr Burton-Summerhayes indignantly. She stood up to make clear that the interview was at an end. 'The vaccine is perfectly safe and quite essential,' she said firmly.

The one skill she had acquired in her years as a doctor was the ability to end a conversation without the listener being in any doubt that the conversation had ended. 'I agreed to see you as a gesture of sympathy in view of your family loss. But I don't see any point in our continuing this discussion. You are, I'm afraid, merely looking for someone to blame for what has happened. The vaccine that was given to your son has saved millions of lives and, if he hadn't been given that vaccine, the chances are that your son would have been killed by covid.'

Mr and Mrs Mallory stood up. Mrs Mallory took a handkerchief out of her bag and wiped her eyes.

'If you believe so much in the vaccine why are you hiding at home?' asked Mr Mallory. 'Is it true that you aren't seeing patients because you are worried about catching covid?'

'How dare you question my working practices?' demanded Dr Burton-Summerhayes.

Mr Mallory stared at the doctor for a moment and then put his arm around his wife's shoulders and led her out of the room, out of the health centre and back into a world which now seemed dark and empty of hope.

When Mr and Mrs Mallory had gone, Dr Burton-Summerhayes sat back down, quietly fuming. She remembered why she didn't see patients face to face anymore. Patients were, she thought, so utterly unreasonable and demanding. How dare these people question her judgement? And relatives, she thought to herself, could be worse than patients.

She wondered how much longer she'd have to wait before she heard about the job with the drug company.

Mrs Mallory wrote and made formal complaints, as she had said she would, to the General Medical Council and the National Health Service.

Two weeks later she received formal, rather stilted and dismissive letters telling her, in no uncertain terms, that they were rejecting her complaints out of hand.

'Doctors all agree that the covid vaccine is perfectly safe and effective,' said someone from the General Medical Council.

'There is no reason to suspect that your son's death had anything to do with his vaccination,' said a bureaucrat replying on behalf of the National Health Service.

Mr and Mrs Mallory even went to see a lawyer at a firm which specialised in medical negligence cases. The lawyers didn't charge a fee but took a percentage of whatever damages were awarded.

'Our son was killed by the vaccine,' they told him.

'Which vaccine would that be?' asked the lawyer.

They told him.

'We'd be wasting our time with that one,' said the lawyer with a shake of his head and a sigh. 'There's no chance at all. The drug companies were given immunity from prosecution. We can't sue them or the doctors who authorised or gave the injections. So we'd have to sue the Government. And they'd simply produce an army of doctors to say the vaccine didn't cause so much as a rash or a hiccup.'

He shrugged, put the cap on his pen without writing down any of Mr and Mrs Mallory's details and escorted them out.

And, officially at least, that was that.

And then Mr Mallory had a heart attack.

He was at home when it happened, sitting in the living room and watching a football match on the television.

Mrs Mallory found him when she took him in a mugful of coffee and his biscuits.

Mr Mallory usually drank tea, the standard breakfast tea, not one of those expensive fancy teas named after people or places, but the sort of tea workmen prefer, served strong with a dash of milk for the sake of tradition, and two sugars, but on a Saturday afternoon he always had a large mugful of hot, black coffee and with it he always ate two chocolate digestive biscuits. Neither he nor Mrs Mallory could remember when or where or how this small tradition had started but, as the years totter by and you get a little older, even the smallest of traditions take on significance beyond their apparent value.

And so, when she heard from the television set that the game had reached the half time point (the moment when Mr Mallory liked to have his coffee and biscuits, as though he were sharing with the players those few moments of respite from the physical and mental stress of the sporting rough and tumble) Mrs Mallory took her husband his mug of coffee and, as prescribed, two chocolate

digestive biscuits on a plate. Mrs Mallory was not the sort of woman
who ate or served biscuits straight from the packet.

And she found him slumped in his chair, ashen faced and gasping
for breath, looking like a man more in need of an ambulance and the
full panoply of modern medical care, than the woefully inadequate
mug of coffee and plate of biscuits (chocolate covered digestives
though they were) which Mrs Mallory was carrying.

Mrs Mallory was not a woman to panic on the outside, though she
was certainly panicking on the inside, and she was not the sort of
hysterical woman found in films; the sort who can always be relied
upon to drop a tray full of crockery and scream at a moment of
surprise. Instead of screaming and dropping the tray she put the mug
of coffee and the plate of biscuits down on the small coffee table
which stood beside Mr Mallory's chair, precisely positioned and
ready and waiting to serve in this way and, although she felt her
heart beating rather too quickly for comfort, she tried to remain
calm.

'What is it, love?' asked Mrs Mallory, taking her husband's hand
in hers and feeling for his pulse. His hand felt clammy. When
working in the care home she had tried to learn as much as she could
about doctoring and nursing. She was accustomed to being the first
person on the scene in an emergency.

In response, Mr Mallory clutched at his chest. There were beads
of sweat on his forehead. 'It's easing off a little,' he whispered. 'I'll
be fine,' he added. He didn't want to worry his wife. Indeed, if he
had died there and then he would have died worrying not about his
own mortality but about upsetting his wife.

'I'll get some aspirin,' said Mrs Mallory who, in her years as a
care home assistant, had seen enough heart attacks to know one
when she saw one. She hurried to the kitchen, found a packet of
soluble aspirin, pushed two tablets out of the plastic pack and took
them back into her husband. 'Put these under your tongue,' she said,
popping the tablets into his mouth.

'Under my tongue?'

'Just let them dissolve there. They'll be absorbed more quickly.
They'll help dissolve any blood clots in the arteries round your heart.
Dr Naylor told me that,' she said. 'When he was alive,' she added,
wishing for a moment that he was still available. He would have
been there with them, with his battered old Gladstone bag and his

old-fashioned stethoscope, much larger than any other doctor's. There was, she remembered, a patch on the stethoscope tubing where it had perished slightly. It was one of those patches normally used for bicycle tyre inner tubes.'

Mr Mallory moved his tongue about until the aspirin tablets were underneath it.

'Sit there and don't move,' said Mrs Mallory quite unnecessarily. 'I'll ring the doctor.'

The doctor's phone was connected to an answering machine which clicked into action after a dozen rings. 'Thank you for your call. Please note that we do not deal with emergencies at this practice,' said a voice which Mrs Mallory recognised as belonging to one of the receptionists. 'If you have an emergency please telephone for an ambulance, or make your way to the Accident and Emergency Department of your nearest hospital. You can find a list of local hospitals online. Please go to our website to rate our service on TruthPilot with whom we are trusted partners. Your call is important to us.'

Mrs Mallory telephoned the emergency number and spoke to a kindly sounding woman who asked her, as calmly as if she had all the time in the world, if she wanted the police, the fire brigade or the ambulance service. Mrs Mallory asked for an ambulance.

'There is currently a waiting time of 16 hours for an ambulance,' said the woman to whom she next spoke. 'Our ambulances and crews are very busy with other calls. We always endeavour to provide the public with the very best service possible. Your call is important to us.'

'My husband is having a heart attack,' said Mrs Mallory. She described her husband's symptoms.

'In that case I can put you on our special emergency list for priority calls,' said the telephone operator. 'I'll check on the availability of that service.' There was silence for a moment. It seemed to Mrs Mallory to last about a month, though in reality it may have been shorter. 'We hope to get an ambulance to you in 17 hours,' said the receptionist, sounding very pleased with herself. 'But I must warn you that the junior doctors and the consultants are all starting their combined strike in 12 hours' time so by the time we can get you to the hospital there won't be any doctors available. Is there anything else I can help you with, today?'

Mrs Mallory thanked the operator and put the phone down. Her first thought then was to telephone Leigh and to ask him to take them to the hospital in his van. And then she remembered that she couldn't ever telephone Leigh again. She suddenly felt very lonely. They had no other relatives. She tried to think of a neighbour she could ask but couldn't think of anyone whom they knew well enough and who would be available. She opened a little personal directory she kept by the phone. It contained the telephone numbers of a plumber, an electrician and a taxi company. She rang the taxi company.

'I'm sorry,' said the woman who answered the phone. 'But we can't get anyone to you this week.'

'It's an emergency,' said Mrs Mallory. She explained.

'Oh, in that case I'm afraid we can't help you at all,' said the woman. 'Our insurance doesn't allow us to carry people who are ill.' There was a pause. 'I'm terribly sorry,' she said, in a mechanical sort of way, the sort of insincere apology someone in a hurry might make after a slight collision on a crowded pavement. 'I'm sure you understand, it's company policy. We can't allow our drivers to be placed in a difficult situation. Our company policy is to ask you to ring an ambulance. But we hope to be of service to you in the future. We are partners with TruthPilot, the internationally renowned ratings organisation. Please go to our website if you would like to leave a rating and a comment. We offer a 10% discount coupon to all those who leave a five star rating.' She ended the connection quickly.

Mrs Mallory went back into the living room to see how her husband was doing.

'Someone has scored a goal,' he said. 'Can you see who it is?'

Mrs Mallory looked at the screen and told him. He didn't seem much interested. 'I can't get a doctor or an ambulance,' she told him.

'That's alright,' said Mr Mallory. 'I'd rather stay here.' He looked at his wife and smiled. 'The aspirin seems to have disappeared,' he said.

'That's good,' said his wife, who still had faith in old Dr Naylor, still providing advice from beyond the grave.

'The pain has pretty well gone now,' said Mr Mallory. He turned towards the television set as the commentator's voice rose in volume and pitch, glanced at what was happening and then turned back to Mrs Mallory.

'Shall I make you another coffee?' she asked. 'I expect this one has gone cold.'

'Just pull up a chair and sit with me a while,' said Mr Mallory. 'Turn the TV off. I've rather lost interest in the match.'

Mrs Mallory looked at him and knew he was ill. He loved his football. She moved the little table out of the way and moved a chair so that they could sit beside each other and hold hands.

'I'll look after you,' she whispered to him. 'We can deal with this together.'

'I know you will,' said Mr Mallory. 'I know we can.' He squeezed her fingers.

'I'll read up about what we should do,' she said. She took a hanky out of her cardigan pocket and wiped away an impertinent tear which had appeared uninvited in the corner of her left eye. 'I'll find out what sort of diet. I'll look into how much bed rest you need; when you can start exercising and how much exercise you should take. I'll find out if you need any pills.' She stopped and thought for a moment. 'Perhaps we should carry on with the aspirin every day. Just a low dose would be enough. And I'll keep you away from stresses and strains. That's important.' She turned to her husband but his eyes were closed. She felt for his pulse. It was now regular, steady and strong. His breathing was fine. She took a fresh tissue from the box and wiped his forehead again. And then she just sat beside him, watching and listening. It was, she thought, that bloody vaccine again. The doctors would say that it was just a coincidence that her husband's heart attack had occurred so soon after his covid-19 vaccination. That was what they always said. There was a global epidemic of coincidences. The establishment, in all its various forms, always defended the vaccine but there had, she knew, been thousands of coincidences in recent months. Thousands of healthy, young adults had died, healthy, young adults just like her Leigh. And then there were the strokes, and the cancers that had come back out of the blue, and the infections and the unexplained bleeding and the palsies and the miscarriages.

Her husband wouldn't be having any more vaccinations, of that she was certain. She'd murder anyone who went anywhere near him with a needle and a syringe.

Mr Mallory didn't take any pills, other than the daily small dose of aspirin which his wife gave him to help prevent any clots developing around his heart, but slowly and surely he got better. As much as she could, his wife protected him from the stresses and strains which are an inevitable part of life in the 21st century; she put him on a low fat diet (oven cooked chips once a week as a treat) and gave him plenty of salads and fresh fruit. After a week or two, when he was definitely looking and feeling healthier, they went out for a walk in the local park and slowly they increased the time they spent exercising.

There were a few scares, of course. Once or twice, Mr Mallory had some mild pains in his chest, and once he had pain in his left arm (and that, Mrs Mallory knew, was much the same as having a pain in your chest as far as the heart was concerned) but the pains gradually diminished in severity and the length of time they lasted.

'I always knew, right from the start, that the covid vaccine wasn't safe, like they said it was,' said Mrs Mallory one day. She and Mr Mallory were sitting on a bench in the park, watching children feed the ducks.

For a while Mr Mallory didn't say anything. One of the children, a small boy, nearly slipped into the pond as he hurled a crust of bread into the water with especial vigour. He was aiming to drop the piece of bread close to a solitary duck which was hanging back from the others. The boy had to be pulled back from the edge by an older girl, a sister perhaps. The children were all laughing.

'Leigh used to love feeding the ducks when he was little,' Mr Mallory said at last. 'Do you remember we used to bring him here on Saturday mornings? He used to look forward to it so much.'

'I remember,' said Mrs Mallory softly.

'Do you really think it was the vaccine that killed him?'

'I do. I'm certain of it.'

'Another boy from the cricket club dropped down dead last week. He was just 18-years-old. That's four deaths now – all among men under 30. And there have been two deaths among the football club players. That's not natural. It can't be natural.'

'Do you know the flu disappeared completely in 2020?' said Mrs Mallory. 'And the number of people who died from covid was almost exactly the same as the number who used to die from the flu?'

'I read that,' said Mr Mallory. 'And I read that the total number of deaths in 2020 was no more than the total number of deaths than usual. What sort of a pandemic is it when there are no more deaths than usual?'

They sat quietly together for a while. A little sunshine filtered through the clouds and warmed their bones.

'I could kill that bloody GP,' said Mrs Mallory in a whisper.

Mr Mallory looked at her. He couldn't remember the last time he'd heard her swear. He put his hand on top of hers.

'I wonder how many people they've killed with that vaccine,' said Mrs Mallory, to herself as much as to her husband. 'I read something the other day showing that hundreds of thousands of young, healthy adults and children have been killed by it. And still they insist that it's harmless.'

'At least they're admitting now that the vaccine doesn't stop people getting covid,' said Mr Mallory.

'Oh, they've said that for a long time now. It doesn't do what they said it would do but it does kill people.'

'People like our Leigh.'

'People like our Leigh and the other boys in the cricket club and the football club. And it very nearly killed you, too,' said Mrs Mallory.

They sat for a little longer and then, when the children had gone and the sun had disappeared behind a large cloud, they walked back home.

'Nice cup of tea do us both good,' said Mrs Mallory.

On their way home they stopped and bought two fresh teacakes from the local bakery.

When they got back home they found that the postman had been.

'You sort out the mail while I put the kettle on and toast the teacakes,' said Mrs Mallory.

There wasn't much mail to sort out.

There was a letter from their electricity company inviting them to have a smart meter fitted, a letter from a company offering to triple glaze their home (and promising a discount if they allowed the company to take photographs to use in their advertising brochure) and a letter which Mr Mallory recognised as coming from the health centre.

Mr Mallory tossed the first two letters into the rubbish bin (the senders had generously if unwisely advertised the contents on the envelope so he didn't have to waste time or energy opening them) and opened the third envelope with slightly trembling fingers. He was always nervous when he opened a communication from the doctor.

'What is it, dear?' asked Mrs Mallory, slicing two teacakes into halves.

'They've given me an appointment for next Thursday morning. They want me there at 9.15 am,' said Mr Mallory. 'But they say that I should allow the whole morning for the appointment.'

'For your hip? Oh that's wonderful. That's much faster than we expected. I wonder what happened. Do you think it helped that I telephoned and spoke to the consultant's secretary?'

'No, love, it's not about my hip. They want me to have another covid vaccination. The letter says that if I don't have another injection my vaccination certificate will expire and I'll be treated as if I haven't had a vaccination at all.'

Mrs Mallory stopped watching the toaster and turned to her husband. She reached out and put her arm around him. 'Even if you were prepared to have it done, their certificate doesn't matter at all now, does it, love?'

'Not in the slightest,' said Mr Mallory. His heart attack meant that he had to take time off work and since he had been unable to provide a doctor's note (the doctor wasn't available for appointments or the signing of sick notes) or say when he would be back, the boss had 'let him go'. Mr Mallory always thought that was a curious phrase. It made him feel like a balloon. Still, it wasn't as bad as the other phrase employers always used: 'we're letting you go so that you can explore new opportunities'.

Nothing, no promises, and no threats, would have persuaded Mr Mallory to allow himself to be injected with a vaccine which was, he firmly believed, responsible for their son's death and his own heart attack. And if Mrs Mallory had, for one moment, feared that her husband might have kept the appointment (an unlikely eventuality to be sure) she would have knocked him down, tied him to the bed and locked the bedroom door.

They ate their buttered, toasted teacakes and drank their tea and then Mr Mallory telephoned the health centre and left a message on their answering machine; giving his name and the time of the appointment, and declining their kind invitation.

And then they sat for a while, neither of them saying anything but both of them thinking a great deal.

It was Mr Mallory who broke the silence. 'They're not going to stop, are they?'

'No, they're not.'

'How many people do they want to kill?'

'As many as they can.'

'These are evil people.'

'The people behind it are evil,' agreed Mrs Mallory. 'But the people who give the vaccinations, the doctors who do the jabbing, or who tell a nurse to do it for them, are just ignorant.'

'And greedy. I read that they get paid far more for giving the covid vaccine than for any other vaccine.'

'Some of them are making an extra £50,000 a year simply for turning a blind eye to the truth – and for telling their nurses to jab everyone in sight.'

'Do you think that Dr Burton-Summerhayes knows that the vaccine is killing people?'

'I don't think she knows anything. She doesn't even know it doesn't work. She just knows how much she gets paid to go along with the lie. Like most of them she hides behind the Government and the drug companies and lets them fill her bank account with cash.'

'We have to do something,' said Mr Mallory after a while. 'How many other parents are going to lose their children?'

'And they're killing the old people too,' said Mrs Mallory. She pulled the four slices of tea cake from the toaster and put them on two plates. 'This vaccination programme was never designed to protect people. It was designed to kill people.'

'And it's killing millions.'

'It will kill billions in the long run. I've seen enough evidence to know that the vaccine destroys people's immune systems. People will die of quite ordinary infections because their bodies can't protect them.'

Mrs Mallory took the butter from the fridge and a knife from the drawer and then started to butter the teacakes. 'And Dr Burton-Summerhayes killed our Leigh.'

'Without people like her prepared to do their dirty work for them the people behind the vaccine wouldn't be able to do anything,' said Mr Mallory. 'The vaccine would just sit in their warehouses. It's the doctors who have to be held responsible.'

'But what can we do? We tried complaining and they brushed us off.'

'We tried to sue them and the lawyer said it wouldn't be possible,' said Mr Mallory. He popped teabags into two mugs and poured boiling water on top of the tea bags. He took a jug of milk out of the fridge and put that and the sugar bowl on a tray along with the two mugs.

'I got the impression he thought it was unfair that we couldn't sue. I think he thought we ought to have had the right to sue them.' Mrs Mallory, holding a plate in each hand, led her husband into their living room.

'I think lawyers are probably always disappointed if they can't sue somebody.'

'That's true,' agreed Mrs Mallory.

'They ought to take all the doctors who gave the vaccine to court. They were in breach of doctors' ethics. They completely ignored every medical ethical code in existence – going as far back as the Hippocratic Oath and including principles of medical practice which were established at the Nuremberg Trials.'

'I thought the Nuremberg Trials were just for war criminals.'

'They were, but a lot of doctors were tried and the trial established some basic principles for medical practice. The doctors who gave the covid vaccine were giving an experimental vaccine but the vast majority didn't tell their patients it was an experiment and so they certainly didn't obtain their permission. That was in breach of what was decided at Nuremberg.'

The two of them sat down, ate their teacakes and drank their tea. They didn't speak.

'Do you want another cup of tea, dear?' asked Mrs Mallory after a long, long while.

'That would be nice.'

Mrs Mallory stood up. 'I'll take these things out into the kitchen and put the kettle back on. Those teacakes were lovely weren't they? They make a lovely treat.'

I could kill that doctor,' said Mrs Mallory, finishing her second cup of tea.

It wasn't the first time she'd had the thought. And it wasn't the first time she'd turned the thought into words.

'It would save a lot of lives if we did,' said Mr Mallory.

'She wouldn't give out any more covid jabs.'

'I could kill her, too,' said Mr Mallory quietly. 'She didn't care. She didn't give a damn. She didn't want to care. She didn't want to know.'

His wife looked at him.

There had been no anger in his voice, just as there had been none in hers, just a quiet sadness and a soft determination. He said it in the same unemotional way that he might have said 'I think I'd like an egg for my tea' and after he had spoken she realised that the thought they had shared had not been an idle one.

They allowed the thought to simmer for the rest of the evening.

They weren't violent or even angry people. Mrs Mallory couldn't remember the last time her husband had lost his temper. And although she was a determined woman who didn't like to see anyone being treated badly or unfairly, Mr Mallory couldn't remember the last time his wife had raised her voice. They had always been kind, generous and gentle people. They were the sort of folk who used to be described as 'the salt of the earth'.

But they had loved their son Leigh very much indeed.

And he had been taken from them by people who simply didn't care and who had expressed no regrets and no remorse.

It was the following day when the subject reappeared, though neither of them had slept well.

'So,' said Mr Mallory at breakfast time, 'what are we going to do about it?'

Mrs Mallory spread marmalade on a piece of buttered toast and finished what she was doing, making sure every square inch of the toast was neatly covered before she spoke.

'We have to do something,' she said, at last.

'We do. If we let them go on giving the vaccine then a lot more people are going to die.'

'We can't kill all the doctors.'

'No. But we can make a start. Not picking up a piece of litter because you can't possibly pick up all the litter isn't much of an excuse.'

'No, it isn't.' Mrs Mallory, who was still holding her knife, started to re-spread the marmalade then, realising what she was doing, she put down the knife and picked up her cup of tea.

'I never imagined I'd seriously think of doing anything like this.'

'No,' agreed Mrs Mallory. She put down her cup, though she had not taken even a sip. Neither of them needed nor wanted to spell out what they were talking about.

'But it seems the right thing to do.'

'Yes. It does.'

They talked for a while and within an hour they knew what they were going to do. Since the toast and the tea had both gone cold, Mrs Mallory made a fresh supply of both.

That evening, after their supper, Mrs Mallory telephoned her sister Leonora who lived 90 miles away. The distance meant that they didn't see much of each other but despite this they were very close. Leonora was married to an estate agent and lived in a large, Victorian house in the smartest part of the town. ('Estate agents always have the nicest houses,' explained Leonora one day. 'They get to see properties as soon as they come onto the market and they know when someone is desperate to sell and will accept an offer.') The couple had no children of their own and thought of Leigh as their own. Two or three times during the season, Leonora's husband would drive over to sit with Mr Mallory and watch Leigh play cricket. Leonora, who worked as a counter assistant in a pharmacy, would travel with him and the two sisters would spend the day shopping and catching up with each other's news before driving to the cricket ground just before the tea interval.

'Are you OK, love?' asked Leonora. 'Sorry, that's a stupid question. Of course you aren't. We still can't get over the fact that Leigh has gone. We loved him so much.' She tried, unsuccessfully, to stifle a sob. 'He was a like a son to us.' She blew her nose and, for the sake of her sister, tried to compose herself.

'Can I pop over and see you tomorrow?' Mrs Mallory asked her sister.

'Of course you can, my love! Are you both coming? Can you stay the night? I'll make one of those steak and kidney puddings you both like.'

'It'll just be me this time,' said Mrs Mallory. 'And only a flying visit I'm afraid.'

'Has something else happened? Is George OK?'

'George is fine. I just need to see you for a minute or two. But I need to see you at the pharmacy.'

'Really? Now you have intrigued me. Are you poorly?'

'No, we're both fine,' said Mrs Mallory. 'Well, you know…as fine as we can be. What's your quietest time of the day?'

'Well, Mr Parkinson takes a long lunch these days. He drives out to the golf club and he's usually gone from one until nearly three. He likes to keep the shop open so I bring a sandwich and a flask. I don't mind. He's very good about letting me off early or about taking the day off if Leigh is playing in a match.'

Suddenly realising what she'd said Leonora started to cry.

'I'm sorry,' she said after a minute or two. 'That's the last thing you want.'

'That's OK,' said Mrs Mallory softly.

'We're usually pretty quiet between two and three,' said Leonora at last.

'I'll see you tomorrow, just after two,' said Mrs Mallory.

'Is this a good moment?' asked Mrs Mallory, having waited until the only customer had decided that she didn't want to buy a hot water bottle after all. There was no one else in the shop.

'What's up, love?' asked Leonora.

'Do you keep a stock of the covid vaccine?'

'Of course we do. We've got more of that stuff than anything else. The doctors are still jabbing everyone who keeps still for more than ten seconds. They're making a fortune and Mr Parkinson does very well out of it too. If it weren't for the covid jab we'd probably have to close now that the big chemist in the High Street has expanded. One of the doctors in Bedworth Street has just bought himself an Audi and his wife a new Mercedes – one of the really big ones. And a young GP at the health centre behind the old Woolworth's has bought himself a Porsche. Very flash. Bright yellow.'

'The vaccine killed our Leigh,' said Mrs Mallory, suddenly.

Leonora looked at her and nodded quietly as though this wasn't much of a surprise. 'Really?'

'We're sure of it. They've hushed up thousands of deaths. It's been mainly young men who've been dying, but lots of young women have died too. And an awful lot of children and teenagers have died or been made ill. They're blaming the deaths on everything except the vaccine. One doctor on the television said people were dying because of global warming. Another said they were all dying because they were eating the wrong food. Someone else blamed vaping. And someone else said it was because they weren't taking enough exercise.'

'Those doctors on the television do talk such rubbish!' said Leonora. 'And I'm fed up with all the talk about global warming. It's global warming this and global warming that. And it's been a rotten summer. We had two week's holiday in August and it rained virtually every day.'

'They said our Leigh developed myocarditis and died of heart trouble. But you know Leigh. He was as fit as a fiddle.'

'Just a few weeks ago, I saw his picture in the paper with the football club.'

'They gave him a trophy as their player of the year. He scored more goals than anyone else last season. He had chickenpox when he was seven, when everyone in his class had it, but I can't remember him ever having anything else wrong with him. Then they give him the covid jab and within days he was dead. If it was only Leigh I wouldn't be so sure but there have been thousands of other young people dying. And lots of middle aged people suddenly dying too.'

'I had heard rumours,' said Leonora. 'One of the doctors was in talking to the pharmacist. They said there were a lot of problems but no one liked to talk about them. I heard them talking about a cover-up.'

'They knew before they started giving it that it wasn't safe,' said Mrs Mallory. 'There was evidence. I've seen it. They published a list of the side effects they knew that the vaccine would cause. And myocarditis was on the list.'

'Someone ought to expose it,' said Leonora.

'People have tried. But all the doctors who have spoken up have been silenced. They won't let them speak out. They say that anyone who criticises the vaccine is a dangerous conspiracy theorist. They call them discredited so that no one will listen to them.'

'Well, someone needs to do something,' said Leonora. 'It's not right.'

'Where do you keep your vaccines? The covid ones?'

'In the back with all the other medicines. Oddly enough they don't officially count as dangerous drugs, though from what you say they kill more people than anything else. Because they're not officially 'dangerous' we don't have to keep them locked up with the opiates. We used to have to keep them in the fridge but then they changed their minds about that.'

'So they could be stolen quite easily?'

'What on earth do you want covid vaccines for?'

'Never you mind! It's best you don't know.'

And Leonora, being a wise and good sister, did not pursue the point. 'To be honest, the pharmacist would be quite pleased if someone did steal some of them!' she said. 'We've got 76 boxes of them that are out of date. I don't know why we got sent so many. When they arrived the pharmacist said that most of them would go out of date before we could use them – and they have. I suppose the Government paid for them all with our money. Now they've got to go back to the wholesaler. I keep bumping into the boxes.'

'What does the wholesaler do with the out-of-date vaccines?'

'Dispose of them somehow. Burn them in an incinerator. Crush them for landfill. I don't really know. They're out of date so they have to be destroyed. I expect they have to burn them because they'd be a biohazard wouldn't they? They can't be used though they're probably no more dangerous than the replacement batch we just had brought in. That's why the pharmacist is fed up – we've got several dozen boxes of the new vaccine which have just come in and we've still got the old, out-of-date vaccines, waiting to go out.'

'Do they check all the boxes when they take them away? Check to see what's in them?'

'Oh no. We had to return a batch six months ago and they just counted the boxes. No one cares what's actually in the boxes as long as they have the right number of boxes.'

And so ten minutes later, Mrs Mallory said goodbye to her sister and left the pharmacy with 100 vials of out-of-date covid-19 vaccines and a rather large, disposable plastic syringe in her shopping bag. Back in the pharmacy one carefully resealed cardboard box, now carrying less than its advertised complement of vials, sat with 75 other boxes awaiting collection.

On her way home, Mrs Mallory called in at the care home where she had once worked and, from a friend still working there, she obtained a litre of saline in a plastic bag and a giving set suitable for providing fluid and drug therapy for a patient.

'Oh darn it,' she said, when she showed her husband what she had collected. 'We haven't got a drip stand. I could have borrowed one.'

'What's a drip stand?' asked Mr Mallory.

'It's a metal stand, about five foot something high which stands by a patient's bedside so that you can hang a drip bottle on it. The stands usually have little wheels on the base so that they can be wheeled round.' Mrs Mallory looked very cross with herself. 'How could I forget that?' She thought for a moment. 'I suppose we could hang the bottle on a lamp or a picture rail.'

'It's a bit risky, hoping that there will be a standing lamp. And very risky hoping for a picture rail in a hotel these days.'

'Oh bother! What are we going to do? I'll have to pop back to the care home tomorrow.'

'Are the little wheels essential?'

'Not for us they aren't. Not at all. We're not going to be moving the drip stand. And neither is Dr Burton-Summerhayes. She's not to be wandering around to the television room, or having a walk round the ward to find someone to chat to. She's going to be lying flat on her back on her bed.'

'A five foot tall metal stand is going to be a little cumbersome,' said Mr Mallory. 'Wouldn't it be difficult to carry?'

It would stick out like a sore thumb,' agreed Mrs Mallory. 'People would notice someone carrying a drip stand.'

'And they don't collapse, I don't suppose.'

'No, I don't think so – which is a pity. A collapsible drip stand would be perfect.'

'Then I've got just the thing,' said Mr Mallory.

He disappeared and a few moments later came back with a cardboard box about two feet long. As his wife watched he opened the box and took out several lengths of metal piping, a tripod, obviously intended to be used as the feet and a bracket designed for hanging bird feeders full of peanuts and sunflower hearts.

'That's perfect!' said Mrs Mallory as her husband put the bird feeder together. 'Just what we need.'

'We can take it into the hotel in a small suitcase. And when we've finished with it we just take it apart again and it'll fit back into the suitcase.'

Dr Burton-Summerhayes looked around her hotel suite with quiet satisfaction. It was, to say the least, luxurious. On one table there was a bowl of fresh fruit, on another there was a vase of fresh flowers, with a note signed by the hotel manager hoping that she would enjoy her stay at the Langford Country Hotel. A neatly displayed array of top end magazines lay on a third table, together with a bottle of Bollinger champagne cooling in an ice bucket. Alongside the ice bucket stood two crystal flutes. A notice on top of the refrigerator informed her that all beverages and snacks within were complimentary and that complementary teas and coffees were available 24 hours a day from the staff of the hotel's room service, who would also be delighted to provide complimentary sandwiches and meals 24 hours a day. In the bedroom there was a box of chocolates on the bedside table and on a second, larger table that day's newspaper, pristine and neatly folded in a paper wrapper, and a free iPad (with the compliments of the host drug company) which contained an app containing details of all the company's products. There was a note informing her that she was free to take the luxurious full-size bath robe away with her at the conclusion of her stay. It was a pity, she thought, that she hadn't had anyone to bring with her to share the champagne and other goodies.

Dr Burton-Summerhayes wondered how much all this was costing the drug company picking up the bill. The company was paying for her and a dozen other GPs to spend a luxury weekend in what was, she had been assured by the drug company's representative who had invited her, one of the most expensive hotels in England. All she and her colleagues had to do in return for this lavish hospitality was to attend a short lecture about the company's most popular heart drug.

The seemingly surprising and (officially) unexplained explosion in the incidence of myocarditis and heart disease, particularly among previously healthy, young men, meant that the already massive market for the drug was exploding. She'd read somewhere that the company was expecting to see its profits improve by several billion dollars simply from the increase in the sales of its best-selling heart drug, and all a result of the increase in the number of patients needing treatment for heart troubles. She wondered if it were true that the drug companies had known how much damage the covid vaccine was going to do and had ramped up the production of heart drugs in order to take advantage of the increased market. The thought of it made her smile. Some people regarded such thinking as wicked; she simply regarded it as good business, pre-planned opportunism.

Dr Burton-Summerhayes selected an orange from the fruit bowl, sat down in a chair by the window and used a fruit knife to peel the piece of fruit, using a pristine copy of *Country Life* magazine as a tray. She left her matching, unlocked suitcases (brand new, genuine Louis Vuitton pieces which were free gifts from the organisers of a drug company weekend which had been held at the Ritz hotel in Paris) where the porter had put them (the £1 coin she had given him would be her one expense for the weekend) having been assured that the housekeeper would open her cases and put her clothes away.

Once again she wondered how long it would be before she heard whether her job application had been successful. She was terribly excited at the prospect of leaving general practice and taking a job in the drug industry, where there was so much money to be made. The interviewer she had seen had spoken of a seat on the board within three years at the most, and there had been talk of huge bonuses and share options. No promises had been made but it hadn't been idle chit-chat and if they wanted her, which she felt sure they would, she could hammer all that out in the contract. She wondered if she ought to find herself an employment lawyer, ready, willing and able to help her with the negotiations.

While Dr Burton-Summerhayes was eating an orange, enjoying the luxury of her extravagantly equipped suite and dreaming of a future with a huge salary, an unlimited expense account and a trouble-free life of drug company sponsored and well-paid indolence (free of the sort of irritations which she had concluded were inevitably associated with having to deal with patients, let alone their relatives), Mr and Mrs Mallory were, by absolutely no coincidence whatsoever, making themselves as comfortable as possible in their budget, bottom of the range, cheapest available room on the very top floor of the same hotel.

Their room had originally been intended for use by hotel maids, but since the hotel staff now insisted on superior accommodation in specially built residential quarters, the attic rooms had been converted to what the hotel referred to as 'affordable luxury accommodation for discerning travellers on a budget.'

And while Dr Burton-Summerhayes enjoyed complimentary flowers, chocolates and champagne (and a complimentary bar), Mr and Mrs Mallory had to be content with a complimentary, plastic shower cap and a small, plastic bottle of complementary, hypoallergenic shampoo, two small packets of biscuits on a plastic tray, an electric kettle (complete with two cups and saucers and a variety of hand-picked teas and coffees plus minute, plastic pots of milk and sachets of sugar), a fridge containing an array of vastly overpriced beverages and peanuts, and a large, clearly printed, and rather stern, notice warning customers that the luxurious, full size bath robes provided for the use of customers were available for purchase at the hotel reception desk and that the hotel management would regard any attempt to remove bathrobes, towels or other items as theft.

'Now, have we got everything,' said Mrs Mallory, as they emptied their small suitcase (cardboard, Woolworth's circa 1967) and checked what they had brought with them. Mr Mallory described each item as Mrs Mallory checked a little list which she had written on the back of an old envelope. Mrs Mallory had sprinkled confetti in her hair for their arrival and had told the receptionist that they were on their honeymoon. They had decided that this would explain why they did not move from their room and were not seen taking advantage of the hotel facilities.

'Box of vaccines.'

'Check.'

'Pair of two-way radios with new batteries. Both radios are working.'

'Check.'

'Bird feeder.'

'Check.'

'Litre of saline.'

'Check.'

'Giving set with plastic tubing and needle.'

'Check.'

'Roll of micro-porous non-allergenic surgical tape.'

'Bag of bungee cords.'

'Check.'

'Rubber, surgical gloves. One pair large. One pair small.'

'Check,' said Mrs Mallory, folding the used envelope and putting it back into her handbag. 'And that's it.'

Mr and Mrs Mallory were ready. They had everything they needed.

Mr and Mrs Mallory and Dr Burton-Summerhayes did not meet up until late that first evening.

Mr and Mrs Mallory had stayed in their room all day, unwilling to wander around the hotel in case Dr Burton-Summerhayes saw them and recognised them.

Dr Burton-Summerhayes, on the other hand, had had a busy day. Between 11.30 am and 12.00 noon there had been a lecture, given by an eminent cardiologist who was receiving a fee equal to a month's pay, on the extraordinary qualities of the company's favourite heart drug. After a splendid five course luncheon in the hotel dining room (a special area of the dining room had been cordoned off for the doctors and they had the best view of the gardens, the heated outdoor swimming pool, the tennis courts and, in the distance, the golf course) Dr Burton-Summerhayes had sat by herself in the hotel lounge, reading old copies of *Country Life* magazine and trying to decide whether she would purchase a country estate or a large apartment somewhere within walking distance of Harrods when her drug company bonus and share options had been safely gathered in.

At 4.00 pm, while she enjoyed a cream tea and the first of several pre-dinner liqueurs, Dr Burton-Summerhayes spoke for a while with a senior drug company representative. He invited her to attend a lecture (rather grandly described as a long weekend educational conference) at the Cipriani Hotel in Venice. She would, he told her, be travelling there and back in a private compartment on the Orient Express and while in Venice she would have a pre-paid gondola, together with gondolier, at her disposal. She happily accepted the invitation, put a note in her diary and made a note to arrange to take off the Thursday, the Friday and the following Monday. Since she would be attending an educational conference, there would be absolutely no trouble in arranging her absence with her partners and she would receive a large fee from the State health system in recognition of her dedication to improving her knowledge.

Half a dozen of the GPs present had gone off to play golf on the hotel's private course and didn't bother to attend the drug company presentation. Dr Burton-Summerhayes, however, knew that the drug company representatives who were present would be watching, and that those doctors who didn't bother to turn up for the half hour lecture would probably not be invited to any more luxury weekends. She very much enjoyed the luxury weekends and tried to spend every weekend as a guest of one or another of the major pharmaceutical companies. She had very little in the way of a social life, and absolutely no hobbies or interests, and some of the doctors and nurses with whom she worked were impressed by what they thought was her total dedication to her work.

In the evening, Dr Burton-Summerhayes attended a seven course evening dinner, complete with three different types of wine, where she sat between a very boring and more than slightly drunken GP, who put his hand on her knee every time he spoke to her, and a charming and attentive senior regional sales representative from the host drug company. She eventually managed to ignore the GP so completely that he turned his attentions to one of the waitresses, a buxom girl in her twenties who giggled a good deal, and when the doctor wrote his room number on a corner of the menu, tore it off and handed it to the waitress, who was not inexperienced in such matters and was saving up for a holiday in Cornwall, slipped the piece of the menu inside her dress so skilfully that one or two of those present did not notice what had happened.

After the dinner there had been coffee and liqueurs in a private lounge, where those visiting doctors who weren't sitting at the bar doing permanent damage to their livers (at the expense of the host drug company) had been entertained by a once famous but now rather faded television star who sang old songs, told old jokes and oozed well-worn professional charm.

When the entertainer had gone to bed (with a magnum of champagne and a young waiter), and she had finished her fourth liqueur, Dr Burton-Summerhayes had tottered, more than slightly tipsy, back to her room. It was as she headed back to the lifts, that Mrs Mallory, now sitting, well-hidden behind a palm tree and a copy of the local evening paper, used her half of their two-way radio set (which she pretended was a mobile telephone) to tell her husband that the doctor was on her way and was, most importantly, quite alone. Mr Mallory, who also pretended that his half of their two-way radio set was a mobile phone, laughed and said that he would see to it straightaway.

Upstairs, having fumbled with the funny little bit of plastic which hotels use instead of keys, Dr Burton-Summerhayes stumbled through the door of her suite and along the small hallway leading into her living room.

The stumble was real because, with impeccable timing, Mr Mallory pushed his way into the room, propelling the tipsy doctor ahead of him and kicking shut the door behind him. The door, as solid as hotel doors ever are, closed with a firm and reassuring click.

The doctor half turned, about to protest to whoever was behind her, but she did not have time to utter a word before Mr Mallory, still pushing her forwards, hit her on the head with the bottle of champagne which had been part of the welcoming package which the drug company had instructed the hotel to provide; a bottle which Dr Burton-Summerhayes, who didn't much like champagne, had been preparing to take home to give to her brother as a Christmas present.

Fortunately for all concerned, Mr Mallory did not hit the doctor too hard and the bottle did not break. The last thing he wanted was an inexplicable damp patch on the carpet and a good deal of broken glass to clean up.

Dr Burton-Summerhayes subsided with remarkable grace and was, a moment or two later, lying flat out on the floor.

Hitting the doctor on the head had not been Mr Mallory's first choice. His original plan had been to 'slip the doctor a Mickey Finn', but this suggestion (which, it must be confessed, had rather appealed to Mr Mallory, who was a fan of the sort of old-fashioned black and white movies where people were regularly 'slipped a Mickey') had foundered upon close examination. Mrs Mallory had pointed out that they would need a supply of chloral hydrate (which they did not have) and that they would somehow have to persuade the doctor to drink the concoction.

And so, rejecting the idea of the Mickey Finn, on the grounds that there were too many imponderables and uncertainties, they'd fallen back on the traditional blunt instrument, agreeing that it could be fitted without difficulty into their slightly adapted scenario and that, moreover, there would be no difficulty in finding a suitable blunt instrument ready and waiting in the doctor's suite. Hotel rooms, particularly luxurious hotel suites, are invariably well-equipped with blunt objects and if, by the strangest of ill fortune there had been nothing suitable available, Mr Mallory had, in his pocket, a hefty copy of the Gideon Bible, which he had borrowed from their room (though only after a short prayer of apology to God, accompanied by the hope that the Good Lord would understand and forgive if not approve.)

The minute Dr Baron-Summerhayes was stunned and on the floor, Mr Mallory used his two-way radio to call his wife, and a bare three minutes after he had made the call he admitted Mrs Mallory to the room.

Mrs Mallory, surprised to realise how calm she felt, stood beside her husband, looking down at the doctor who was lying on her back. Dr Burton-Summerhayes was not looking at her best for she had started to snore and to dribble at the same time. Mrs Mallory was holding in her left hand a small suitcase containing the various essential items which they would need for the next and most important part of their plan. They had, rightly, decided that no one would look closely at someone walking along a hotel corridor carrying a suitcase.

'What if they do a post mortem?' asked Mr Mallory.

'They won't,' said Mrs Mallory. 'Pathologists stopped doing routine post mortems on sudden deaths during the covid hoax. They claimed it was because there was a danger that they'd catch covid and die but it was really so that their post-mortem diagnoses wouldn't interfere with the diagnoses of the doctors who had been enthusiastically writing 'covid-19' on death certificates, even when their patients had died of heart disease or been run over by buses.'

Lifting the unconscious Dr Burton-Summerhayes onto the bed had not been difficult. Mrs Mallory, thanks to her years of work in the care home, had some considerable experience in such matters, and she was able to direct the operation in such a way as to ensure that her husband's recovering heart was not put under undue strain.

Once the doctor was laid out on the bed, Mrs Mallory removed all of Dr Burton-Summerhayes's clothing (Mr Mallory, a gentleman through and through had politely turned away) and then (after a slight struggle) dressed her in an unflattering flannel nightie (the nightie was decorated, Mrs Mallory noted with some surprise, with small colourful pictures of Spanish bullfighters posing amid branches of spring time blossom) which the attentive housekeeper had folded neatly (but not exceptionally neatly since the housekeeper had spoken to the porter who had reported his modest tip) and then placed upon the left hand side pillow of the king size bed with which the suite was furnished. It was the housekeeper's experience that single women invariably slept on the side of the bed furthest from the door when they stayed in a hotel. She assumed that they probably thought it made them safer though whenever she herself stayed in a hotel room she always made the door immoveable by stuffing a couple of thick wedges into the space between the bottom of the door and the carpet.

When Dr Burton-Summerhayes was dressed in her awful nightie (which, thought Mrs Mallory, looked like the sort of nightie an emotionally stunted twelve-year-old might have worn in the 1950s) she and Mr Mallory used the supply of bungee cords which they had brought with them to prevent the doctor moving and to fasten her to the bed. They used the doctor's tights to gag her, to prevent her crying out and to ensure that they were not disturbed. They put two pillows under her head so that she was sitting up and could comfortably see what was happening, and what was about to happen.

The bungee cords had been Mr Mallory's suggestion and now that she saw them in use, Mrs Mallory thought how perfect they were. It occurred to her that, in the unlikely eventuality that she were ever to write a guide book for kidnappers she would definitely recommend the use of bungee cords rather than bits of old washing line; the first big advantage being that with bungee cords there is no need to tie any knots, the second being that they are quick to use and quick to release and the third being that they cannot be unpicked or untied and cannot be cut with the odd bits of glass which kidnap victims in films always seem to find readily available. And although they can be fastened quite tightly they are less likely to cause tell-tale marks on the skin.

It was, both Mr and Mrs Mallory had agreed, an integral part of their plan, quite essential indeed, that Dr Burton-Summerhayes should be alert and awake at the crucial part of the operation and should know precisely what was happening to her and why.

By the time that Dr Burton-Summerhayes had begun regaining consciousness, Mrs Mallory had everything she needed neatly lined up on the bedside table.

'I'm going to remove the gag from your mouth,' said Mrs Mallory. 'If you scream or make an unreasonable amount of noise I'll put it straight back and leave it there.' She pulled the rolled up tights from the doctor's mouth.

'What the devil is going on? Who are you? What do you want?' demanded Dr Burton-Summerhayes; firing out the questions in quick succession as she awoke. She tried to rub her head which was sore but she found, to her horror and astonishment that she couldn't move either arm.

'Do you remember me?' asked Mrs Mallory, carefully moving towards the bottom of the bed so that she was in the doctor's eye line.

'You're that woman who came to see me,' said Dr Burton-Summerhayes, frowning as she tried to remember more. 'Someone died and so you came to the surgery, pretty well forced your way into my consulting room and wanted to blame me for the death.'

'My son died,' said Mrs Mallory quietly. 'You gave him the covid vaccine and he was dead within days.'

'There was probably something wrong with him. A few people with hidden health problems were made ill by the vaccine. Just temporary little problems usually: a headache or a rash'

'Leigh, that's my son, was healthy and strong. He played football and cricket for the town teams. The vaccine killed him as surely as if he'd been shot.'

Mr Mallory took a photograph of Leigh out of his jacket pocket and held it up so that Dr Burton-Summerhayes could see it. 'This is our son,' he said. 'His name was Leigh Mallory and you killed him just as surely as if you'd shot him or stabbed him in the heart.'

'I didn't do any vaccinations,' insisted Dr Burton-Summerhayes. 'None whatsoever. I never give vaccines. Other people do things like that. '

'No, you don't give vaccinations, but you tell other people to give them,' Mrs Mallory pointed out. 'The nurses you employ only give vaccines when you've authorised them to do so. And you made a great deal of money out of the vaccination programme you ran for your patients.'

'My head hurts,' said Dr Burton-Summerhayes. 'Did someone hit me? Why are you letting me see your face? Why aren't you worried that I'll go to the police and have you arrested?'

'You knew people would die, didn't you? You instructed nurses to give an experimental, untested vaccine which you knew would kill people?'

'Of course I didn't know it would kill people! And it was tested. It was tested very thoroughly. There are dangers with all drugs. If you take these straps off me and just leave my suite immediately I'll forget that any of this happened.'

'Don't lie to us anymore,' said Mrs Mallory wearily. 'The covid vaccine was rushed through in weeks when vaccines normally take years to reach patients. And don't lie about forgetting that this ever happened. The minute we leave you'll be on the telephone screaming for the police.'

'You would be able to argue that you were both deeply depressed by the death of your son. I'm sure the courts would be very lenient. If you stop now, you'll probably just be fined. Or maybe given a period of probation or community service.'

Mrs Mallory moved from the bottom of the bed and made her way back to the bedside table. Mr Mallory, taking his cue from his wife, followed her and took the bird feeder out of the suitcase. Within seconds he had put it together and stood it beside the bed.

'The vaccine was essential. It was a global emergency. What on earth are you doing with that? What is it? It looks like a bird feeder!'

'But it wasn't essential was it? It was never essential. Covid-19 was simply the flu. The covid-19 infection was downgraded on March 19th in 2020 when the public health bodies in the UK and the Advisory Committee on Dangerous Pathogens decided that the 'crisis' infection should no longer be classified as a 'high consequence infectious disease'. The country's leading experts looked at covid-19 and decided that it was no more dangerous than the flu.' Mrs Mallory hung the bag of saline on the top hook of the bird feeder.

'They had to be ignored. They had to be overruled. There was a risk that millions would die.'

'They were just a small group of scientists. They had to be ignored. What are you doing with that saline? You're going to be in very serious trouble if you don't let me go.'

'No, they didn't have to be ignored,' said Mrs Mallory. She connected the giving set tubing to the bag of saline. 'The people who made that decision weren't just any old group of scientists. They were the people regarded as the most knowledgeable in the country – the public health bodies and the Advisory Committee on Dangerous Pathogens. And they decided that covid-19 wasn't the threat the politicians said it was. Afterwards, we heard a good deal from a good many so-called experts. Some of them were just mathematicians working with computer models of no value whatsoever. One of them, whose name I forget, had a terrible track record. He had been making inaccurate predictions for years. Many of them were making all sorts of absurd and scary statements in order to get two minutes on the evening news. But the media ignored the real experts who had decided that covid-19 was no worse than the flu. It was the job of the Advisory Committee on Dangerous Pathogens to decide whether covid-19 was or was not a serious threat. They decided that it wasn't a serious threat. And they were over-ruled by the politicians because their conclusion was inconvenient. Governments all around the world wanted a crisis; they wanted a global pandemic; they wanted to create fear. And they over-ruled their own advisory committee so that they could do just that.'

'None of that was my fault!' said Dr Burton-Summerhayes, whose voice had risen noticeably. 'You can't hold me responsible for what happened. I was told by the Government's advisers that the vaccine was essential and safe. If they were wrong then that was their responsibility and they should be held to account. What are you planning to do what that needle?'

'It's going to go into this nice plump vein just here,' said Mrs Mallory, taking hold of the doctor's right hand and tapping a large vein on the back of her hand. 'I'll use this vein, rather than one in the crook of your elbow, because no one will notice a mark just here. The bruising will cover it up.'

'What bruising? I don't have a bruise. What are you doing?'

'There will be some bruising there, believe me, there will be some considerable amount of bruising on the back of your hand.' She slid the needle, which was connected to the giving set, into the vein and turned on the plastic tap to check that the fluid flowed through satisfactorily. She then turned off the plastic tap. 'I'll tape the needle in place so that it doesn't slip out but this is hypo-allergenic tape so you won't have a rash.' She tore two strips off the roll of microporous tape which was in her case, and used the two strips to fix the needle into the back of the doctor's hand. 'We don't want a rash there, do we? If someone sees it afterwards they might wonder what caused it.'

'Stop this at once!' demanded Dr Burton-Summerhayes furiously.

'The people you were listening to were all compromised,' said Mrs Mallory. 'In America, the Government's medical adviser had links to the vaccine industry. And in the UK, the Government's Chief Scientific Officer had previously been employed by a major drug company and vaccine maker. He was employed by them for years and while he was there the company was repeatedly fined for behaving dangerously and irresponsibly.'

'You can't blame me for any of that! I'm just an ordinary GP.'

'Yes, I can blame you for what happened. You should have asked questions. You had the authority to recommend and give the vaccine. With authority comes responsibility and you had a responsibility to make sure that the vaccine was safe and necessary.'

'Lots of leading doctors said we should give the vaccine. All the medical journals recommended that we give the vaccine.'

'The leading doctors were being paid by the drug companies. And the world's medical journals are all bent. They make millions out of drug company advertising. When did one of the medical journals last criticise the drug industry? The medical journals charge big subscription fees – they should live on those fees and prove their independence.'

'All medical journals carry drug company advertising. It's how they survive. And advertising is an essential way for drug companies to let doctors know about their new products.'

'By advertising new painkillers and heart drugs like bars of chocolate or soap powder? If doctors were still members of a profession they would be embarrassed or even humiliated by the way drugs are promoted. Did you look at any independent evidence?'

'What independent evidence? There wasn't any. We all had to rely on the Government.'

'There was plenty of real evidence – if you'd bothered to look. The real experts knew that the vaccine would cause horrendous problems. When we saw you in your consulting room I told you that in December 2020, before you started giving the vaccine to patients, the Food and Drug Administration in the United States published a draft working list of the very serious problems the covid vaccine could cause. The Old Man in a Chair made a video listing the side effects – side effects which included myocarditis and dozens of other major health problems. If he knew about the risks then you should have known about the risks.'

Mrs Mallory used a syringe to draw up the contents of one of the vials of vaccine. She injected the vaccine into the bag of saline. She repeated this small operation a couple of dozen times, putting the empty vials back into the suitcase.

'What are you doing now?' demanded Dr Burton-Summerhayes, twisting her head to try to see what happening.

'I'm injecting the covid-19 vaccine into the saline which is going to flow into your veins in a couple of minutes' time. I'm giving you around 100 times the regular dose of the vaccine. If you believe in the vaccine then you'll be very well protected against covid, won't you?'

'You aren't doctors. You don't understand. The vaccine was essential. It was needed to save lives. There was a real danger to the nation's health. The world was in peril. Do you have any idea what will happen if you allow all that vaccine into my blood stream?'

'In peril? Really? You can't be so stupid that you believe that nonsense. And yes, I think I know what will happen when the vaccine enters your blood stream.'

'Hundreds of millions of people were killed by covid. The death toll would have been much higher without the vaccine. I was helping to save lives.'

'If you had bothered to look at the number of deaths in 2020 and 2021 you would have seen that there were no more deaths in those years than there are in any average year. All you cared about was that you were making tons of money. As far as you were concerned it was all just about money.'

'Why are you doing this to me? You can't hold me responsible for everything you think was wrong about the vaccine! It's not fair.'

'We don't hold you responsible for all the harm the vaccine did,' said Mr Mallory, speaking for the first time in a while. 'We're doing this because you killed our son. You were greedy and negligent and you are responsible for his death.'

'This won't bring back your son!'

'No, of course it won't. Nothing will bring back our son.'

'So, why are you doing it? I can give you money, a good deal of money, if you take that needle out of my vein.'

'I'm afraid we're doing this for two rather straightforward and old-fashioned reasons,' said Mrs Mallory. 'We're doing this out of revenge. And so that you won't give deadly vaccines to any other patients.'

'And not all the drug companies in the world have enough money to pay for what you did,' said Mr Mallory.

'I heard that you tried to sue me,' said Dr Burton-Summerhayes. 'The solicitor you saw spoke to a friend of mine. You must have wanted money.'

'No, we didn't want to sue you because we wanted money. We just wanted to expose the truth.'

'Revenge won't help you. It won't make you feel any better. It won't get you anywhere. It's a very negative emotion.'

'You're right about that,' said Mr Mallory. 'It won't bring back our son. But we'll feel a little better about it. You'll be dead. And you won't be able to give vaccines to anyone else.' He thought for a moment. 'The trouble was, you see, that the pain you caused was just too much – that and the sense of frustration and powerlessness that went with it.'

'And the arrogance of you vaccine-loving doctors made things worse,' added Mrs Mallory. 'By denying the truth and sneering at anyone trying to share the truth, and by suppressing the evidence which you should have been sharing, you increased our sense of fury and frustration.'

'Another doctor will authorise the vaccine if I don't! You won't make any difference. And you'll spend the rest of your lives in prison.'

'Maybe they will. And maybe they won't. But I don't think anyone will catch us or send us to prison. Your death will be put down as a Sudden Adult Death. And that's ironic isn't it?'

'What do you mean?'

'Well, the term Sudden Adult Death Syndrome was invented as a cover diagnosis, a label to put on all the deaths caused by the vaccine. The authorities refuse to acknowledge that the vaccine can kill people and so they need a scapegoat diagnosis – hence there is now a global epidemic of deaths caused by Sudden Adult Death Syndrome. They may suspect that you died because you had a covid jab but they'll never accept that –so you'll be officially listed as having died from Sudden Adult Death Syndrome. I have to admit that SADS is going to make it very easy to murder people. The more times someone has been given the covid jab the more likely they are to drop dead unexpectedly – and to be labelled as just another Sudden Adult Death Syndrome victim. Even you have to admit that there are a couple of layers of irony there.'

'You're very stupid people,' spat Dr Burton-Summerhayes. 'You're doing this just to frighten me? You won't dare kill me.'

Mrs Mallory fully opened the plastic tap which controlled the flow of fluid through the giving set tubing and which allowed the vaccine enriched saline to flow into Dr Burton-Summerhayes's body.

'Do you have any idea what you're doing?' demanded Dr Burton-Summerhayes, trying hard to look down at the back of her hand and then sideways up at the litre of vaccine enriched saline.

'Oh yes,' said Mrs Mallory with confidence. 'I know exactly what I'm doing. I know more about this toxic vaccine than you knew about it when you arranged for one of your nurses to inject the stuff into my son. From what I know, I think you'll start with neurological symptoms – some paralysis, perhaps. And you'll start to feel very hot and itchy. It's quite possible that you will have an anaphylactic shock reaction – in which case everything will be over very quickly. This vaccine is a very dangerous substance. If there is no anaphylaxis then there will possibly be some clotting in your veins and the chances are that you'll have a heart attack or some other serious heart problem. Our Leigh was very young and healthy and he only had a single vaccination but he developed myocarditis which killed him very quickly.'

Dr Burton-Summerhayes died long before all the saline enriched vaccine had entered her bloodstream. It was, of course, impossible for either Mr or Mrs Mallory to determine the cause of death, but there was no doubt that the doctor was dead. In due course there would doubtless be a funeral, though probably not a memorial service. There wouldn't be many tears and the eulogies, if there were any, would probably be short and taken off the peg rather than taken from the heart.

The minute she was satisfied that the doctor was dead, Mrs Mallory turned off the tap on the giving set, peeled off the two pieces of micro-pore tape which had held the needle in place and carefully removed the needle from the back of the doctor's hand. She put all these, together with the remains of the saline and the giving set into a plastic ziplock bag which she placed in her suitcase. Mr Mallory dismantled the bird feeder and added that to the suitcase. They then unfastened all the bungee cords, checked that the cords had left no marks on the doctor's skin, and added the cords to the case.

Mr and Mrs Mallory then half lifted and half dragged Dr Burton-Summerhayes off her bed and moved her into the bathroom. Mr Mallory soaked two towels in water and dropped them onto the marble tiled floor (their own, much cheaper room, at the top of the hotel had linoleum on the bathroom floor) and the pair of them then pulled the dead doctor to her feet, positioned her carefully and then banged the back of her hand on the side of her bath. Then they lifted her to her feet again before letting her fall so that her head hit the side of the basin. A solitary piece of soap, suitably dampened, and placed on the floor, provided the final touch.

'There we are,' said Mrs Mallory, standing back a couple of feet and checking the scene of the accident. 'She came into the bathroom, slipped on a wet towel or the piece of soap and she fell. As she fell, she hit the back of her hand on the side of the bath and her head on the rim of the basin. Deaths like this happen all the time. When I worked in the care home we had at least one death a year like this – and we had non-slip floors.'

Once they had set the scene, Mr and Mrs Mallory sat quietly in the sitting room and waited. They did not eat any of the fruit or drink any of the contents of the bar. And they didn't open the champagne.

At 3.45 am, having decided that this was the time when the hotel corridor would be at its quietest, they opened the door, checked that there was no one about and then, with Mr Mallory carrying their suitcase, walked back up the emergency staircase to their room. Once they were safely inside their room, they removed the rubber gloves they had worn throughout and then ate the two packets of sandwiches which they had brought with them and which, although a little stale, were very welcome. They used the kettle in their room to make two cups of tea. They then undressed, washed, cleaned their teeth and got straight into bed. For the first time since Leigh had died, they both slept very well.

The next morning, Mr and Mrs Mallory ate their breakfasts in the hotel dining room. There was now no reason for them to hide since there was no chance of Dr Burton-Summerhayes spotting them, recognising them and wondering what they were doing in the hotel where she was staying. No one had yet found the body of Dr Burton-Summerhayes and it seemed unlikely that anyone would find it for several hours at least. And Mr and Mrs Mallory were pretty confident that when someone did find her, there would be very little fuss made. (They were sorry for the maid who had to find the body but there was no way round that.) Mrs Mallory was certain that they had set the scene very well. Large, exclusive hotels don't like to draw attention to unfortunate deaths on their premises. 'Who should we deal with next, do you think?' asked Mr Mallory, speaking quietly as he began work on his traditional English breakfast. He never ate a full English breakfast at home but always did in hotels. 'Who will be the next covid-19 vaccine promoter to die unexpectedly of Sudden Adult Death Syndrome.'

'Oh, what about that smarmy Dr Mike Rainbough, the oh-so-smooth television doctor?' suggested Mrs Mallory. 'He was on television almost every day during the worst days of the hoax and I've never heard anyone tell so many lies. He made Boris Johnson sound like a choir boy.'

'He'll be on my short list to be dealt with quickly,' agreed her husband. 'How could anyone trust a doctor who owns so many immaculate, expensive Savile Row suits and has £200 haircuts?'

'I saw in the paper that he's just been selected to appear on that BBC show 'Synchronised Swimming with the Stars',' said Mrs Mallory. 'There was a picture of him practising in his swimming pool at home.'

'And he's just published the first three of a series of books which a ghost writer put together for him. I can even remember the titles: 'Bowels for Beginners', 'Livers for Learners' and Arthritis for Amateurs'.'

'I must remember to get them from the library,' said Mrs Mallory drily.

'And we need to deal with that creature Hancock. What's he doing these days?'

'The last I heard he was presenting a radio show for the Cheepy Chappy supermarket chain. No one listens to him but apparently his droning voice puts shoppers into a hypnotic trance. The supermarket keeps him on air because people end up filling their trollies with more soap powder and loo rolls than they intended to buy.'

'And don't forget Whitty – that funny looking doctor, the independent Government spokesman with links to Gates the amateur vaccine enthusiast.'

'We mustn't ignore that mathematician whose absurd predictions started off the whole scare. What was his name? He had a terrible track record but they believed him because he told them what they wanted to hear.'

'And there's that woman. She was all over the news, filmed getting standing ovations every time she went anywhere. What was her name?'

'Elspeth Warthy-Botham,' said her husband. 'Elspeth Warthy-Botham.' He paused and repeated the name. 'I bet I can guess what they called her at school.'

'That can't really be her name?'

'Oh, I think it is.'

'And we need to see that doctor at the hospital. He was horrid. He didn't give a damn about Leigh.'

'I think he should be dealt with very soon. And Rancid Reynolds, the lead singer of the Sauteed Kidneys band has to go onto the urgent list. He was the one who said he wouldn't let fans into his concerts unless they had been vaccinated. And he did a series of pro-vaccine TV ads for the Government.'

'Oh, we'll definitely visit him! He was one of the people who influenced our Leigh.'

'And then it will be time to head across the Atlantic,' said Mr Mallory. 'There's a lot of work to do over there.'

'Don't worry, I hadn't forgotten them,' agreed his wife. 'There will be quite a few people to see in North America – both in the United States and in Canada. We'll start with that awful Mr Gates, deal with the terrible Dr Fauci and then work our way through the mass of toxic neoliberals who promoted the covid vaccine with such misplaced enthusiasm.'

Mr Mallory finished the last of his toast and emptied the remains of his morning coffee. The breakfast which the hotel served hadn't been at all bad.

'The bags are already in the car boot,' he said. 'I'll pay our bill and then we'd better be on the road. We've got a lot of planning to do. And if they haven't all gone back to the wholesaler yet maybe you could get another couple of boxes of those out-of-date vaccines from your sister.'

Later that day, Dr Burton-Summerhayes left the hotel in a body bag, precariously balanced on a trolley. She was taken downstairs in the service lift and removed to the undertaker's plain van via the service entrance. There were no witnesses to her departure.

The hotel doctor, a local GP who was available for emergencies and sudden 'incidents', confirmed the death as 'accidental' ('another bar of soap and a wet towel on marble floor' he said to the assistant manager) and the solitary policeman who was called to investigate confirmed to the hotel's assistant manager that the coroner would be assured that there was nothing to investigate.

Dr Burton-Summerhayes would never know that a registered letter was on its way to her, offering her the drug company job she so desperately wanted.

What a pity.

The Author

Dr Vernon Coleman MB ChB DSc has been writing about drug companies and the medical profession for over 50 years. His first book 'The Medicine Men', published in 1975, was the first to question the relationship between the drug industry and the medical establishment. Since then he has written over 100 books (including many international bestsellers).

In February 2020, he told readers of his website www.vernoncoleman.com that the risks associated with the coronavirus were exaggerated. At the beginning of March 2020, he explained how and why the mortality figures had been distorted. On March 14th 2020, he warned that the Government's policies would result in far more deaths than the disease itself.

In a YouTube video recorded on 18th March 2020, Dr Coleman warned that governments would use the fake 'crisis' to oppress the elderly, to introduce compulsory inoculation and to begin to replace cash with digital money.

He revealed that the infection had been downgraded on March 19th when the public health bodies in the UK and the Advisory Committee on Dangerous Pathogens decided that the 'crisis' infection should no longer be classified as a 'high consequence infectious disease'. Just days after the significance of the infection had been officially downgraded, governments around the world put millions of people under house arrest.

Dr Coleman was immediately banned from all social media (Facebook told him he could not join because he would be a threat to their 'community'). Publishers banned his books and articles. YouTube deleted his 'Old Man in a Chair' channel, removed videos with millions of views and even banned him from looking at other people's videos. He was demonised, lied about and libelled.

Throughout 2020, Dr Coleman issued a series of videos (often one a day) detailing the dangers of the covid-19 'vaccine' and produced a number of books including 'Coming Apocalypse', 'Covid-19: The Greatest Hoax in History', 'Endgame', 'Social

Credit: Nightmare on Your Street', 'Proof that Face Masks do more Harm than Good' and 'They want your money and your life'. His other books include 'Anyone who tells you vaccines are safe and effective is lying: Here's the Proof' and 'How to stop your doctor killing you'.

Dr Coleman, a former GP principal, is a Sunday Times bestselling author. His books have sold over three million copies in the UK, been translated into 26 languages and sold in over 50 countries. Prior to March 2020 he had published over 5,000 articles and papers in newspapers, magazines and journals and had written columns for dozens of leading newspapers and magazines around the world. He was the founding editor of the British Clinical Journal and founded and published the European Medical Journal. Numerous TV and radio series have been based on his books. His novel 'Mrs Caldicot's Cabbage War' (about the oppression and mistreatment of the elderly) was turned into a highly successful, award winning film. In the UK, he has given evidence about the pointlessness of animal experimentation to the House of Commons and the House of Lords and his campaigns have over many decades changed Government policy. He has lectured doctors and nurses in numerous countries.

Printed in Great Britain
by Amazon

30201138R00036